HELLO, HAPPY!

AN ACTIVITY BOOK FOR YOUNG PEOPLE WHO SOMETIMES FEEL SAD OR ANGRY

Kane Miller

A DIVISION OF EDC PUBLISHING

Kane Miller
A DIVISION OF EDC PUBLISHING

First American Edition 2018
Kane Miller, A Division of EDC Publishing

© 2017 Studio Press
Consultant Dr. Sharie Coombes, Child, Family & Adult Psychotherapist,
Ed.D, MA (PsychPsych), DHypPsych(UK), Senior QHP, B.Ed.
Written by Stephanie Clarkson
Illustrated by Katie Abey
Designed by Rob Ward

First published in the UK in 2017 by Studio Press,
an imprint of Bonnier Books UK

For information contact:
Kane Miller, A Division of EDC Publishing
PO Box 470663
Tulsa, OK 74147-0663
www.kanemiller.com
www.edcpub.com
www.usbornebooksandmore.com

Library of Congress Control Number: 2017942234

Printed in China
6 7 8 9 10

ISBN: 978-1-61067-709-7

HELLO, HAPPY!

THIS BOOK BELONGS TO

Kyleigh M

WELCOME TO HELLO, HAPPY!

Consultant
DR. SHARIE COOMBES
Child and Family Psychotherapist

We all feel sad and angry from time to time, and this fun activity book is a great way to get you thinking and talking about the things that make you feel upset, so you can get on with being you and enjoying life. The pages show you how to push sadness and anger away and will give you ideas about how to feel better.

Use this book in a quiet, relaxed place where you can think and feel comfortable. The activities will help you understand your feelings, feel calmer, talk to others about your worries (if you want to) and grow in courage and positivity. It's up to you which pages you do, and you can start anywhere in the book. You can do a page a day if that's what you want, or complete lots of pages at once. You can come back to a page many times. There are no rules!

Sometimes the things that make us sad and angry can feel really big, and we think nothing will help, but there is a solution to every problem. Nothing is so big that it can't be sorted out or talked about, even if it feels that way. You could show some of these activities to important people in your life to help you explain how you are feeling and to get help with what is upsetting you. You can also always talk to an adult you trust at school or home, who can take you to the doctor to get some help.

Lots of children need a bit of extra help every now and then, and there are organizations you can turn to if you don't want to talk to people you know. They have helped thousands of people with every imaginable problem and will know how to support you without judging you.

CRISIS TEXT LINE

Serves anyone, in any type of crisis, providing access to free, 24/7 support.
Connect with a trained crisis counselor to receive free, 24/7 crisis support via text message. Text HELLO to 741741

www.crisistextline.org

NATIONAL SUICIDE PREVENTION LIFELINE

24/7, free and confidential support for people in distress. Call free or chat online.
No matter what problems you're dealing with, whether or not you're thinking about suicide, if you need someone to lean on for emotional support or are worried about a friend or loved one call the Lifeline.
www.suicidepreventionlifeline.org
1-800-273-8255

HEAD AND HEART

We all have emotions. Happiness, sadness, anger, fear, surprise and disgust are basic instincts - reactions to chemicals being released in our bodies and brains.

Emotions are very useful because they influence the way we behave. For example, if we feel afraid, we try and get away from the danger. If we feel happy, we relax. While our ancestors relied on their emotions to help them stay alive, today we can use emotions to help us manage and plan our lives.

Emotions can change quickly, but the good news is that we can work on and even direct our feelings. Feelings result from emotions and are specific to you. They depend on:

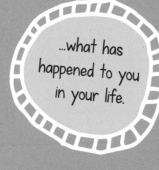

...what has happened to you in your life.

...the way you feel about yourself.

...your temperament and how you deal with emotions.

While emotions are fleeting chemical reactions which cause short-lived physical changes throughout the body, feelings can last for hours, days, weeks, months or even years.

We have emotions from the time we are tiny babies. At first we react to them with simple facial expressions or actions like smiling, laughing or crying. As we grow up, we become better at knowing what we are feeling and putting the feeling into words.

Learning to recognize our emotions in this way and learning to manage the resulting feelings is very important. It's called "emotional intelligence," and it helps us to build relationships, resolve arguments and move past difficult feelings.

Reading this book and doing some or all of the activities will help you to make friends with your emotions and learn to deal with your feelings, so that you can stay happy and positive.

So come on, what have you got to lose? Turn the page and say, "Hello, happy!"

I'M FEELING KINDA...

How are you feeling? Whether you're angry, sad or full of joy, it's OK. All emotions are OK – which is a good thing, as we have lots of them!

Grab a pen and draw the expression to fit the emotion, or add the emotion to fit the expression.

I'M FEELING

Happy

I'M FEELING

angry

I'M FEELING

embarrassed

I'M FEELING

....

I'M FEELING

Sad

....

I'M FEELING

....

embarrassed

shocked

frustrated

angry   shy

scared

lonely   tired

anxious

I'M FEELING

shocked

....

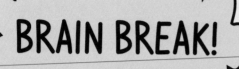

BRAIN BREAK!

To listen to your emotions and feelings you need to quiet your mind. Give your brain a break by switching off from the everyday things which buzz around cluttering up your head.

The first thing to do is to get rid of the noise around you and learn to like silence. It may feel uncomfortable at first, but here's what you need to do:

Turn off the TV.

Turn off any video games.

Turn off any radios or stereos.

Put smart technology (phones, tablets, etc.) away.

Close windows to the outside world so you can't hear car engines and sirens.

Take yourself away from people talking.

Once you've done this...

Sit in a comfortable position, close your eyes and concentrate on breathing in and out, in and out.

Now, in this quiet, calm state, ask yourself how you are feeling.

Give yourself the chance to recognize any underlying feelings of anger, sadness, worry or unease, and give yourself permission to feel that feeling.

For example, say,

"I am feeling SAD. I feel SAD because I had a bad day at school. I will not always feel SAD, but right now I feel SAD and that is OK."

Repeat this several times.

FEELING FEELINGS

Sometimes your feelings don't want to stay inside. Sometimes they want to **BURST OUT.**

Write where and how you feel when you're angry on this drawing.

Write where and how you feel when you're sad on this drawing.

MY BEATING HEART

Take some time to get to know your heart rate. Take your pulse by holding the two fingers nearest your thumb to your neck or the underside of your wrist.

Like all emotions, anger releases chemicals in your brain, which then cause changes in your body that you can feel. One of these changes is an increased heart rate.

TRY TAKING YOUR PULSE WHEN YOU HAVE...

JUST WOKEN UP

RUN IN PLACE FOR 3 MINUTES

HAD A FIGHT WITH SOMEONE

EATEN A BIG MEAL

JUST BEGUN A HOMEWORK ASSIGNMENT

READ A CHAPTER OF A BOOK

BEEN FOR A WALK

Write down your heartbeats per minute for each of these.

REMEMBER! Anger can be positive. Many people have made good changes in the world because they felt angry about something and used that anger to spur them on to positive action. What makes you angry? How could you make a difference in the world?

DID YOU KNOW? Your heart rate will also increase when you are stressed or afraid.

THE ANGER ICEBERG

Anger never exists on its own – there are always underlying emotions causing it. Add more emotions to the underwater part of the iceberg to show other emotions which might lead to you feeling angry.

ANGER

frustrated

ALONE

lonely

SCARED

worried

OFF THE RECORD

An increased heart rate is just one of the warning signs that show you're feeling angry. Circle any warning signs you recognize or have experienced.

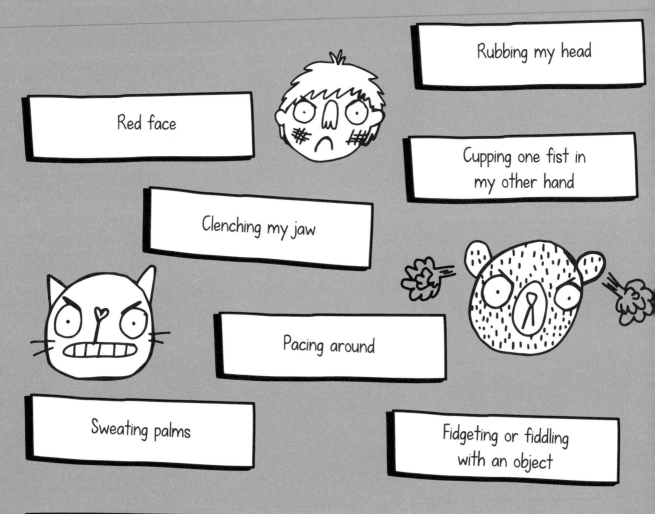

Rubbing my head

Red face

Cupping one fist in my other hand

Clenching my jaw

Pacing around

Sweating palms

Fidgeting or fiddling with an object

Think hard about how you look and feel right before you lose your temper. If you're not sure, ask someone close to you to describe how you look or what you do when you're about to get angry. Learning to spot these signs is vital if you are going to learn to control your temper.

EMOTIONS LTD.

Sadness and anger often go hand in hand.

For example, you might be feeling sad at not having made the soccer team, and as a result, angrily say something mean to a friend who did.

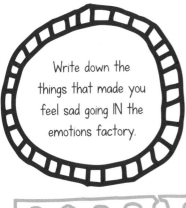

Write down the things that made you feel sad going IN the emotions factory.

If these made you do something in anger, write what you did coming OUT of the factory.

IN

OUT

FACE YOUR FEELINGS

How do you look and feel when an emotion takes over? Pick up your pen, add yourself to the mirrors, then write down the kinds of things you sometimes say or do when you are full of anger or sadness.

Draw how you look when you are feeling angry.

When I am angry I say
...I...hate...you!...
....

When I am angry I
..block..ever-
one out.

Draw how you look when you are feeling sad.

When I am sad I say
....
....

When I am sad I
....
....

ROGUES' GALLERY

How would "anger" and "sadness" look if they were cartoon characters? Use this space and your incredible imagination to bring these key emotions to life.

Are your characters monsters, droopy-eared dogs or crazy-looking plants?

Do they have teeth, fur, scales or feathers?

What are your creatures called? You could name them Angroid and Sadro, or perhaps Gary and Kenneth. Once you've decided, be sure to introduce yourself.

Do they have horns, tails, flippers or fins? What color are they?

What next? Try making your creation from modeling clay.

HOT, HOT, HOT!

Anger can feel like boiling water. One minute it's simmering, the next steam is coming out of your ears. Use the thermometer below and write down examples of times when you've felt different levels of anger.

ENRAGED

FURIOUS

ANGRY

CROSS

ANNOYED

IRRITATED

CALM

SEEING RED

How does the world look when you're angry?

Use shades of scarlet, crimson, magenta, pink, purple and orange to color this picture.

FEELING LOUSY?

What emotions or feelings could these be?

Sometimes other emotions or feelings can stop you feeling happy, and make you feel lousy instead.

ANGER

worry

WRITE OR DRAW TO FILL THIS TRASH CAN
WITH ALL THE THINGS THAT
MAKE YOU FEEL LOUSY!

BULLYING

FLOOD OF FURY

It's important not to keep your anger bottled up until it's out of control.

Imagine the things that make you angry flooding out. Draw or write them below.

Letting anger out in a controlled way will allow it to drain away safely.

TICK TICK BOOM!

The next time you feel like you might explode with anger, try one of these techniques to control your temper, or maybe add ideas of your own.

Once you've tried something, give it a score out of 10 to show how helpful it was.

Anger is a natural emotion. Everyone gets angry, but we need to know how to control explosions of anger. Aggressive behavior is not OK.

/ 10	Bounce really hard on a trampoline.
/ 10	Snap a pencil.
/ 10	Sing to some really loud music.
/ 10	Pummel a cushion.
/ 10	Do 50 jumping jacks..
/ 10	Do a crazy dance.
/ 10	Scream really loudly into a small space, like a cupboard.
/ 10	
/ 10	Scribble really hard in a notebook.
/ 10	
/ 10	
/ 10	Run in place or up and down the sidewalk as fast as you can for 3 minutes.
/ 10	

I'M SO MAD I COULD...

Use your imagination to finish this sentence starter.

...crush a grape.

...HOWL LIKE A WEREWOLF.

...wrestle an octopus.

I'm so mad I could...

I'm so mad I could...

I'm so mad I could...

I'm so mad I could...

I'm so mad I could...

I'm so mad I could...

I'm so mad I could...

I'm so mad I could...

WRITE AND DRAW MORE OF YOUR OWN.

I'm so mad I could...

I'm so mad I could...

I'm so mad I could...

SCRIBBLE-TASTIC!

Feeling *SPIKEY*? Use this page to scribble your anger away.

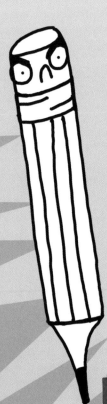

Press as hard as you like –
without going through the paper.

THE FEELINGS FORT

Being alone doesn't have to be lonely. Sometimes if you're feeling angry or sad it's good to have some space.

Why not make yourself a feelings fort – a place where you can go if you want some time by yourself?

You could use chairs, sheets, cushions, or a space behind a desk.

Use the space below to imagine what your perfect hideout would be like.

MY BUGBEARS

Bugbears are things that annoy or irritate you. Write anything that makes you fed up on these bugs. Imagine them flitting away or strolling off into the forest, never to be seen again.

GRRR! I CAN'T BEAR IT WHEN...

COLOR THIS IN

LIFE
CAN BE
GREAT

CLOUD BLOWING

Sometimes it can feel like there's a big black cloud above your head. Next time you feel like that, go outside.

Focus on breathing in the fresh air. Now think of something that has annoyed or bothered you recently.

Pick a cloud and send that thought up to it. Imagine your problem being enveloped in the cloud.

Finally, blow gently out, and imagine the cloud drifting away.

TIME TO LEARN

When we're angry, we don't always think straight. It's useful to learn some techniques to help you feel calmer.

BUDDY BREATHING

Lie down somewhere quiet and calm. Put a pillow or soft toy on your stomach. Breathe in deeply to the count of 2, and then out to the count of 2. Watch as the pillow or toy rises and falls with your breath. Repeat this for 2 minutes.

ARGUING IN FUNNY VOICES

Practice some funny voices or mimic your favorite cartoon characters or celebrities. Next time you're mid argument, try switching to that voice and see what happens.

STOP, DROP, CURL, BREATHE

A good technique to distract yourself from angry feelings is the "Stop, Drop" action. In the middle of an angry episode, tell yourself to stop, then drop down to the floor, curl up in a ball and focus on your breathing. This may seem weird, but if you can do it, it can really help.

KITES

Try imagining memories that make you feel angry as kites. Think about how they may tug at you from time to time, but you have the power to control them. Or, if they are too much, you can simply release the string and let them fly away.

YOU CRACK ME UP

Imagine that your job involves making celebration crackers for your friends and family. Fill the crackers with jokes, stories and funny memories.

GREAT GIFTS

Take some time to think about the people, pets and special friends you love and who love you.
Who would you like to thank in your life, and why?

Write a message on each gift tag.

TO: ....
BECAUSE: ....
....

TO: ....
BECAUSE: ....
....

TO: ....
BECAUSE: ....
....

TO: ....
BECAUSE: ....
....

TO: ....
BECAUSE: ....
....

TO: ....

BECAUSE: ....

....

TO: ....

BECAUSE: ....

....

TO: ....

BECAUSE: ....

....

TO: ....

BECAUSE: ....

....

Write a message on each gift tag.

TO: ....

BECAUSE: ....

....

TO: ....

BECAUSE: ....

SUPER PALS

You might not always think so, but you are super! Just ask your friends. Draw yourself and a friend as superheroes. Think of all your super characteristics.

Write down your super characteristics.
Your friend should do the same on the next page.

Remind yourself why you are friends.

I am ....'s friend because ....

....

.... is my friend because

....

Remind yourself why you are friends.

Maybe you are funny, clever or kind.

If you have trouble thinking of your own super qualities, just swap sides and write about each other!

HELLO, SADNESS

How does your sadness feel?
Use this page to put it into words.

Perhaps it feels like something heavy is sitting on your chest or in your throat. Perhaps it gives you an empty feeling.

WHEN I'M SAD I WANT TO...

Write some words or draw a picture to illustrate the way it feels.

I FEEL LIKE...

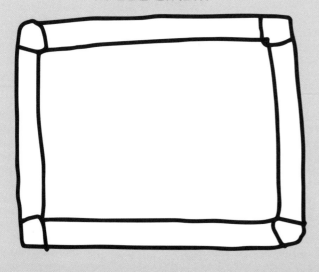

I NEED...

HELLO, HAPPY

Read through these 5 steps, then give them a try.

Did you know you could conjure up some happy feelings for yourself, right here, right now?

1. Lie or sit somewhere comfortable and quiet.

2. Close your eyes.

3. Think about a time in your life when you were really happy about something – maybe you were on a trip, someone was kind to you, or you won a certificate or prize.

4. Try to see yourself at that time – think about what you were wearing, the sights and sounds of the place. How do you feel being there?

5. Hold that picture in your mind for as long as possible.

Use this space to attach a photograph of yourself doing something that made you happy, or draw a picture of yourself doing something you love.

YOU DID IT!
Now that you've aced this exercise, practice it whenever you like, to remind yourself that you can feel happy and to bring a smile to your face.

WHY SO SAD?

Lots of things can make us sad. Look at the pictures and color in any that you've experienced.

MOVING AWAY

NOT FITTING IN

BULLYING

FRIENDSHIP ISSUES

LOSS OF A LOVED ONE

DIVORCE

SCHOOL ISSUES

SHYNESS

Sometimes having to follow the rules can make us feel sad or angry. Cheer yourself up by coloring this picture *outside* the lines or smudging the ink.

MAVERICK MARKS

BALLOON POP

Go on, you know you want to. Pop the balloons
by poking a hole in each with your pencil.

IN A WORD

Can you sum up your feelings or the thing that's bothering you in one word?
If so, fill this page with that word.

Write it big, small, upside down, and backward.

SAD LION, HAPPY LION

This lion is sad. He doesn't like being in a cage.

Use this page to set
him free. Where does
he go? What does
he do?

PILLOW PALS

Sometimes you need a special pal who just listens. Follow the step-by-step instructions to make the perfect pillow pal.

YOU WILL NEED:

One clean white pillowcase
Permanent fabric markers
Scraps of fabric or fleece (optional)
Pins
Scissors (optional)
Needle and thread (optional)
One pillow

WHAT TO DO:

1. Take one clean white pillowcase.

2. Lay the pillowcase on a table or flat surface.

3. Think about the kind of pillow pal you would like – a puppy, a cat, a doll or something else. Choose something you love.

4. Use your fabric markers to draw the eyes, nose and mouth of your new pal.

5. Draw two ear shapes on the reverse side of the scraps of fabric or fleece.

6. Cut them out.

7. Pin the ears where they look best. Sew the bottom parts to the pillowcase. (If you don't have fabric just draw the ears on instead.)

8. Put the pillow in the pillowcase. Your pillow pal is ready for hugs!

Remember! Scissors and needles are sharp.

Ask a grown-up to help with this craft.

Want to do something different?

Why not write the word **Friends** on your pillow and add your friends' names.

Or, ask your pals to write a friendly message to you that you can read whenever you like.

YOU'RE AMAZING!

You may not think so, but you're amazing. Pick the 3 statements which most apply to you.

I am adventurous.

I am a good listener.

I am interesting.

I am reliable.

I am kind.

I am alive.

I am strong.

I am patient.

I am funny.

I am loyal.

I am determined.

I am clever.

I am open-minded.

I am honest.

Write them on the notepaper and repeat them every day.

I am full of promise.

MIRROR, MIRROR

It's hard to feel happy if your self-confidence is low.

Find a mirror, sit in front of it and study yourself.

Find something, however small, that you like about yourself and say it out loud in a confident voice. It could be anything – here are some ideas.

I have thick eyelashes.

I like the way my nose wrinkles when I smile.

My freckles are cute.

My fingernails are a nice shape.

HELPING
HAND

Place one hand on this page and draw around it.

Being kind and helpful to others makes us feel good.

Now's the time to remind yourself of the fact that you're a kind person, and that there are lots of kind people in the world.

On each finger, write down a time when you helped someone.

On the palm of the hand, jot down a time when someone helped you.

Place your foot on this page and draw around it.

WALK IN MY SHOES

When you're really angry or sad, it's easy to feel like you are on your own. But there is always someone who will listen and do their best to understand what you are going through.

On each toe, write the name of someone you can ask for help when you're feeling sad or angry.

END OF THE RAINBOW

Rainbows bring smiles!
What would you love to find
at the end of this one?

DEAR X...

Use this page to write a letter to someone who has made you sad or angry.

When you have finished, tear it out. You can rip it up and throw it away, or bury it in the backyard.

Now that you've expressed these feelings, you can move on.

Today is going to be a good day!
You can sometimes alter your mood and outlook just by thinking positively.

TODAY'S THE DAY

Write down some things you're going to enjoy doing today.

STAIRWAY TO HAPPY

Setting a goal and working toward it is a great way to make yourself feel good.

CHECK OUT
THIS STAIRCASE

Yes, I did it!

I don't want to do it!

Write your goal on the top step. Draw yourself on each step as you move closer to your goal.

SURF'S UP!

Emotions are like waves. They build up, crash over us and then wash away.

Draw the ocean on an angry day.

Now draw the ocean on a calm day.

LITTLE JAR OF AWESOME

1. Find an empty jar with a lid.
2. Decorate it with pens or stickers.
3. Keep it somewhere safe.

Whenever something good, fun or downright awesome happens in your life, write it on a scrap of paper and put it in the jar.

You can open the jar and read the contents on a weekly basis, on a special day like your birthday or New Year's Eve, or whenever you're feeling low.

DITSY DOODLES

It's a good day!
Let your happiness spread across
the page as you doodle.

PAY IT FORWARD

You've probably heard of paying someone back by returning a good deed, but have you ever heard of paying it forward?

This is the idea that you make the world a better place by doing small, random acts of kindness for other people. (Paying it forward makes you feel good too.)

Use this page to think of the ways you could make someone's day.

It could be anything from holding a door open, introducing yourself to the new boy or girl at school, or cleaning out your closet and donating old clothes to charity.

Write positive, kind and lovely messages on reminder notes and stick them up around your house. Your family will feel good and so will you!

FRIENDLY WISHES

Use the spaces here to test out some thoughts before you write them on the sticky notes.

Music can lift your mood. Use this page to make a lyrics poster for a song that makes your spirits soar. Write the words and add some cheery doodles.
Or, write a playlist of all the different songs that help you feel happy.

YOUR TURN!

Use this page to write down words or sentences about your feelings. Can you turn them into a poem or lyrics for a song?

LAUGH IT UP!

When you laugh, your body relaxes and releases endorphins – natural chemicals in your brain that make you feel good.

Think of your favorite animal, then try laughing like you imagine they would: snort like a pig, woof like a dog, caterwaul like a cat, hee-haw like a donkey, screech like a monkey or yak like a hyena.

Imagine yourself laughing at different ages. How did you laugh when you were a baby? When you were three? How will you laugh in ten years? What about when you're eighty?

Laugh like your teacher has just canceled all homework... forever!

Laugh like an evil overlord who's just taken over the universe. Mwa-ha-ha-ha!

Now laugh like Santa Claus.

Grab a friend and a feather duster (or something equally ticklish) and try to get each other to laugh.

Play the "moo" game. Try to make a friend or sibling laugh by moo-ing at them.

WHEN I LAUGH, MY STOMACH FEELS
....
....

MY HEAD FEELS
....
....

MY HEART FEELS
....
....

LAUGH-O-METER

How's your glass today? Is it half-full (feeling mostly hopeful) or half-empty (feeling mostly hopeless)?

	AM	PM
MONDAY		
TUESDAY		
WEDNESDAY		
THURSDAY		
FRIDAY		
SATURDAY		
SUNDAY		

Fill each glass as you go through the week.

Add notes about why you were feeling the way you were on each day.

SMELL AND TELL

Focusing on our senses can help us be in the moment and calm angry or sad emotions.

Play this game with an adult.

Close your eyes. The adult then passes you something fragrant, like a piece of orange peel, or something nice to touch, like a feather.

Keeping your eyes closed, really focus on how the object smells or feels.

You could play this game with a group and take turns to use your senses.

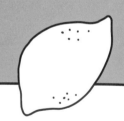

OUT OF IDEAS? TRY ONE OF THESE...

a feather	a sprig of lavender	a piece of spaghetti	some coffee beans
a pinecone	a pebble	a bathrobe sash	a blob of toothpaste
a banana	a plastic piece of cutlery	a cup of rice	a freshly washed piece of laundry
a pencil	a soft toy	a piece of ribbon	a lemon or a lime
a piece of fluff	a rock	a lump of clay	a plastic brick
a rose petal	a deflated balloon	a squirt of perfume on a piece of paper	a leaf
a sprig of rosemary	a shell		

THANKS A BUNCH!

Feeling thankful for the things we have can help us feel better about our problems and worries. Make a thankful tree to remind yourself of the good things in your life.

YOU WILL NEED:

A jam jar or small vase

Stickers or ribbon for decoration (optional)

Long twigs or skinny branches

Pen or pencil

Colored paper

Scissors

Hole punch

String, twine, thread or ribbon

Scissors are sharp! Ask a grown-up to help with this craft.

WHAT TO DO:

You don't have to add all the leaves at once. You could save them to add as you think of more things you're grateful for.

1. First, collect twigs or thin branches. Remember, don't cut anything without permission.

2. Decorate your jar or vase. Add stickers or tie a piece of ribbon around it.

3. Put your branches in the vase, as if they were a bouquet of flowers. Your tree is now ready.

4. Cut leaves from the colored paper.

5. Write down something you're thankful for on each leaf. Then punch a hole in one end of each leaf.

If you don't have a jar or twigs, you can draw your tree on a big piece of paper and stick the leaves on with glue.

6. Tie each leaf to a branch using pieces of string, thread or ribbon.

FILL THIS HEART WITH HAPPY

SAY WHAT?

When's the last time you gave or received a compliment?

Think of some nice things people have said to you and write them in the speech bubbles.

Now think of some compliments you could give others.

JUST A TOUCH OF LOVE

Touch is one of our amazing five senses.

Touch helps us connect with our surroundings and feel better about our world.

Here are some ways to get touchy-feely.

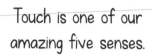

Pet an animal. Maybe you have a pet. If not, ask a dog owner if you can give their pet a pat.

Hold hands with your best friend.

Hug!
Give a friend or family member a squeeze.

Cuddle a fleecy blanket or your favorite soft toy.

Next time you're on the sofa watching TV, ask a parent or caregiver if they'd like a foot massage!

CREATE A CALMING KIT

Imagine always having something to help you feel calm and peaceful. You can easily make a kit to hold all the things that get you feeling happy.

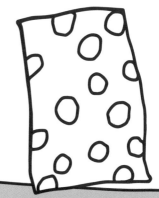

Start by taking a gift box, a shoe box or a little bag. You can decorate it if you like. You'll be using it to store your special things.

Now, hunt around the house to find things you enjoy touching, smelling or hearing. It could even be something you just smile at the sight of.

HERE ARE SOME IDEAS...
WHAT WILL YOU INCLUDE?

a scrap of silky fabric
a small bouncy ball
an old photograph
a scented eraser
a tinkling toy bell
a wrapped piece of candy
a bird's feather

Keep your calming kit somewhere safe. Bring it out whenever you are feeling low, angry or anxious.

ALTERNATIVE ACTIONS

WHAT HAPPENED

One day...

Just then...

In the end...

WHAT HAPPENED

One day...

Just then...

In the end...

WHAT HAPPENED

One day...

Just then...

In the end...

Use the left-hand page to sketch out some examples of times when you were angry and bad things happened as a result. Then, think about other ways you could have acted, and use this page to sketch the difference it might have made.

WHAT I COULD DO DIFFERENTLY

One day...

Just then...

In the end...

WHAT I COULD DO DIFFERENTLY

One day...

Just then...

In the end...

WHAT I COULD DO DIFFERENTLY

One day...

Just then...

In the end...

ANIMAL INSTINCTS

Taking "a walk on the wild side" can help when you're feeling low.

Use this page to think about how you can bring animals into your life.

Taking care of a pet can distract you from negative feelings.

FISHY FRIENDS

Research shows that watching fish swim can have a calming effect. If you don't have your own fish tank, perhaps you could watch fish in a pond or visit an aquarium.

DOG'S LIFE

Dogs are great. If you have a dog, make sure you're first in line to sign up for grooming and dog-walking duties.

PET CARE

Pets take a lot of work, but they're very rewarding. If you don't have your own pet, maybe you could help take care of a friend or family member's companion.

OUTDOOR ANIMALS

Plant flowers for bees and butterflies, or put up a bird feeder to give birds a treat.

FEELING BLUE?

How does the world look when you're feeling sad? Use shades of blue, turquoise, aqua, navy or black to color this picture.

OUT AND ABOUT

Getting out and about can help banish boredom and boost your mood. The next time you're feeling low, grab your coat and head outside.

Check out the ideas on this page and give them a try.

LOCAL LOOKOUT

STOP

Walks are more fun when you've got your super senses attuned to everything around you.

Copy the checklist below on a piece of paper. Make one for each person you're with. Take the papers and pencils and go on a "noticing" walk. Check off each item when you see it.

ITEM	FOUND!		ITEM	FOUND!
Mailbox	☐		Church	☐
Butterfly	☐		Tin can	☐
Stop sign	☐		Cat	☐
Shopping bag	☐		Truck	☐
For Sale sign	☐		Airplane	☐
Goalpost	☐		Rosebush	☐

SOUND SAFARI

Now try a Sound Safari. Copy the checklist below on a piece of paper. Make one for each person you're with.

ITEM	FOUND!	ITEM	FOUND!
Birdsong	☐	A beeping car horn	☐
A dog barking	☐	Someone shouting	☐
The wind	☐	Children playing	☐
The rain	☐	Music	☐
A door slamming	☐	Running footsteps	☐
A fire engine, ambulance or police car siren	☐	A clock or bell chiming	☐

Check off each sound when you hear it.

ONE WORD

Think of your favorite word and write it in the space below. It could be a word that makes you feel happy, or a word that you like the sound of when you say it out loud.

LITTLE JAR OF STRENGTH

Find an empty jar with a lid. Decorate it with pens or stickers.
Every time you think of a strength write it on a scrap of paper
and put it in the jar. Keep it somewhere safe.

GOOD STUFF GRID

Banish bad thoughts at bedtime. Write one hundred things that make you smile on these pages..

You don't have to write them all at once. Just add things when they pop into your head.

Think broadly. Anything goes...

...ice cream, football, walks on the beach, pretzels, furry tigers, mashed potatoes...

SLEEP TIGHT

Getting a good night's sleep can really help your mood. Here's how to give yourself the best chance of some quality zzzzzz's.

NOM NOM

Have a bedtime snack that combines protein and carbohydrates, like milk and cereal, or toast and peanut butter. Don't forget to brush your teeth afterward.

LIGHTS OUT

The healthiest way to sleep is in complete darkness, so turn your lights off. If you don't like the dark, keep your bedroom door open and the hall light on, or use a night-light.

SWITCH OFF AND UNPLUG

Watching TV, using electronics or playing video games before bed is bad news for good sleep. Turn all screens off an hour before bedtime.

BUBBLES AND SNUGGLES

A warm bubble bath and a cozy towel are a great way to help you feel sleepy. Add a bedtime story and you'll be drifting off to dreamland before you know it.

Draw a picture of a dream you'd like to have.

You could base this on a real-life, happy memory or come up with something new.

Remember, it's only a dream! It can be as wild and crazy as you like.

OH THE PLACES YOU'LL GO...

The world's a big place full of endless possibilities.

Write down some of the places you'd like to visit and some of the things you hope to do in the future.

JAR OF LIFE

Making good choices about how to spend your time is really important.

This exercise helps you understand about priorities, and how putting important things first helps make life happier and more fulfilling.

You will need:

A big jar
A bowl of sand
A bowl of small pebbles
A bowl of big rocks

In this exercise:

The jar represents your life.

The rocks represent really important things that money can't buy, like family, friends, good health, goals and doing what you love.

The pebbles represent things that matter, but not quite as much, like homework and your hobbies.

The sand represents things that don't matter at all, like video games, smartphones and holding grudges.

First fill the jar with the sand, then add the pebbles. You will find that you don't have room for all the big rocks.

The exercise shows that if you fill your life with too many of the things that don't really matter, you'll have less room for the things that are really important.

Empty the jar and sort the contents back into sand, pebbles and rocks. Then fill the jar again, but this time with the rocks first, then the pebbles and lastly the sand.

You'll find that the pebbles and sand naturally fill up the spaces between the rocks, and you'll fit much more of everything in the jar.

This shows that if you focus on important things first, your life will be fuller.

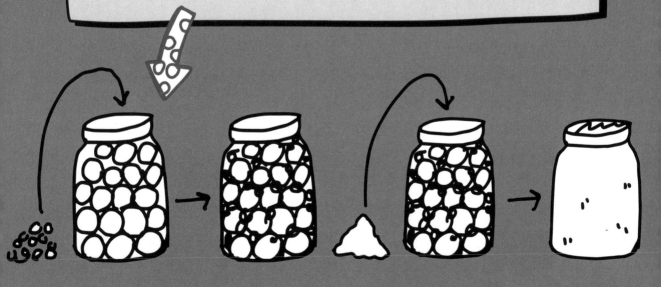

THE PAGE FOR GROWN-UPS

This activity book is perfect for parents, teachers, learning mentors, caregivers, therapists and youth leaders who want to help children to understand and leave behind their worries.

Modern life for our children can be highly stressful, and they can feel like it's all about being popular and successful. We know that they experience many internal and external pressures, for example, comparing themselves with others around them and feeling like they aren't good enough, which can lead to anger.

Children are very resilient, and in a loving and nurturing environment, will often work through problems and difficult times without needing additional help. This book offers the chance for your child to explore, express and explain their worries and open up the conversation with you. The activities foster resilience, increase inner calm, improve understanding of emotions and encourage positivity.

When children feel stuck in sadness or anger, they may become lonely and isolated, and struggle to make sense of what is happening because they don't have the language to explain their distress. You might notice a decline in self-esteem and confidence, along with complaints of stomachaches, headaches or feeling exhausted, as well as an avoiding of previously enjoyed activities.

If your child's distress or anger persists beyond three months or escalates rather than decreases, you can talk to their school, a doctor or a counselor.

NATIONAL ALLIANCE ON MENTAL ILLNESS (NAMI)

Educate, advocate, listen, lead.

The NAMI HelpLine can be reached Monday through Friday, 10 am–6 pm, ET.

NAMI is the nation's largest grassroots mental health organization dedicated to building better lives for the millions of Americans affected by mental illness.

www.nami.org

Tel: 1-800-950-NAMI (6264)
info@nami.org

GOODTHERAPY.ORG®

Helping people find therapists. Advocating for ethical therapy.

GoodTherapy.org offers a directory to help you in your search for a therapist. Using the directory, you can search by therapist location, specialization, gender, and age group treated. If you search by location, your results will include the therapists near you and will display their credentials, location, and the issues they treat.

Tel: 1-888-563-2112 ext. 1

www.goodtherapy.org

CHALLENGE THE STORM™

Sharing stories, resources and support for people facing emotional challenges.

Share your story and express yourself openly, and free from judgement.

www.challengethestorm.org

DR. SHARIE COOMBES